SUSAN LUTE

A Fool For Love

Dedicated to David, a man who loves his classic trucks.

Contents

Preface

Preface

Alice York lived a nomadic life working as a classic car mechanic so she could follow her dream of painting landscapes. When she breaks down in Sellwood, Oregon, and takes a temporary job with sexy Zach Barret, getting drawn into this single dad's delightful family is not in her plan.

Zach Barret has two priorities—be the best dad he can to his twelve-year-old daughter and keep Martha's Elder House running without hiccups, a challenge at the best of times since his granddad persists on chasing off the hired help. When a gypsy caravan-style truck breaks down at Martha's curbside, the last thing Zach needs is an impulsive pixie rocking his boat. The more determined he is to stay away from the free-spirited, green-eyed nomad, the more he finds one kiss is not enough.

Uncovering Alice's secrets in paintings of empty swings and merry-go-rounds puts a new priority in the top spot on his shortlist. But can Zach convince this stunning woman to park her truck permanently in his drive?

Chapter 1

W hen the engine coughed, Alice York swore softly under her breath. Not at her beloved '55 Ford pickup—a classic she'd restored right down to the high-gloss, apple-green paint—but at the timing. The middle of rush hour traffic in Sellwood, a bohemian suburb of Portland, was not the place for the Ford's pampered engine to have a coughing fit.

"Just like a man," she muttered. "Flaking out right when a girl needs him the most. Hadn't expected that from the greatest cowboy in history."

Muscling the ton-and-a-half solid truck with its caravan-style canopy onto a tree-lined side street, Alice sighed in relief when they made it halfway down the block before Duke sputtered to a stop at the curb in front of an elegant, gray Victorian house. An elaborately carved sign read Martha's Elder House.

She slumped in the seat and closed her eyes. She had to get to Dave's Classic Restorations, fifty-five miles away in Longview, where a job working on old classics like Duke waited. With exactly one hundred, twenty-seven dollars and fifty-one cents in her purse, she had barely enough to rent a room and stave off hunger until her first paycheck.

Working on classic cars was good work when she could get it, putting enough money in her pocket so she could make it to her next destination, wherever that might be. And if she was lucky, along the stretch of road ahead of her, she could usually get in a painting or two.

But having to shell out a chunk of her scant reserves for new parts, plus take time to fix the Ford?

She banged her head gently on the steering wheel. She'd had one rule from the very first day she'd taken to the road. A litany of poor-me was not allowed in Duke's cab. Melting into a puddle of panic was not an option.

Hood raised, her head, arms, and shoulders buried in the engine compartment, she tested connections. A door banged behind her with the force of furious anger.

A man's raised voice demanded, "Where are you going?"

Surprised, Alice jerked, hit her head on the hood, and saw stars. "Holy mother of–"

"You don't pay me enough to put up with that old man's insults!" A woman shouted, the voice shrill, pampered. Stilettos clattered past Alice.

Sneakers thumping the sidewalk followed, appearing briefly in her peripheral vision as she rubbed her scalp while blinking back waterworks.

Heavier boots stopped beside the truck. "You can't be serious, Penelope. He's not saying you're a horrible cook. He just likes pushing your buttons."

All Alice could see were denim-clad legs, strong, masculine legs that would make any woman worth her salt salivate.

Chapter 1

What now? Make her presence known? Or pretend she wasn't a witness to this very public domestic squabble.

Staccato beeps released a car lock again and again and again. Two car doors slammed, a high-octane engine roared to life, tires squealed, and the decision was taken out of her hands.

"Lady," the masculine voice sharp with anger now, addressed her. "You can't park that monstrosity here."

Insulted beyond belief, Alice banged her head again and came out fighting. "The Duke is not a monstrosity!"

Dark brows knitted together, lips stretched in a straight line, the man belonging to the heart-thumping man-legs raised his snapping gaze from her backside to her face.

A flash fire of smothering heat burned from said bottom to her cheeks. *Holy mama!*

Her outrage drained while all her girly parts awoke with a shout. *Hello!*

His short, dark hair was painted by the sun with bold blonde streaks. Stormy blue eyes cut her no slack. The unshaven stubble covering a stubborn chin gave him a sexy look that would be hard for any woman to ignore. Alice was nothing but appreciative.

Faced with a long-neglected libido gone wild, she cocked one hip. Folding her arms across her chest, the temptation to trace the line of that stubborn jaw with fingers that itched to explore was hard to fight.

Glaring Sexy Guy probably wouldn't appreciate the grease she'd leave behind unless he liked his casual associations slick and dirty.

"You have to move it." His tone erased any humor her last thought inspired.

His glare didn't intimidate her. She'd seen worse. "Can't."

He matched her stance. "Why?"

"This truck's not going anywhere until I get a new fuel pump."

His glower deepened.

"Dad!" A young girl bounced down the front porch steps, interrupting whatever demand Sexy Guy was about to make. Blonde hair, trapped in ponytails, bounced. "Is Penelope gone?"

"Yes." He noticeably tugged on the reins of his temper for the sake of the child.

Alice gave him a point for good behavior.

"Did she take that creep Blake with her?"

His head snapped toward the girl. It was easy to follow his thoughts.

A sour taste sprang up in Alice's mouth. Had this Blake fellow been a creep to the blue-eyed child with the innocent face?

"Lucy, did Blake—"

The girl shuddered. "Ewe, Dad. No!"

Sexy Guy's shoulders relaxed. Mentally Alice chalked a second point in his column.

He drew a deep breath. "Yes, they're both gone."

The girl pumped her fist, then turned to stare at Duke. "Wow. Cool color."

Her hand, lured by the enticing, shiny apple-green paint, stretched to stroke the truck.

Alice leaned forward to see if the kid had noticed the road winding through the cityscape she'd painted last month on the length of that side of the truck.

She raised an eyebrow. Lucy cocked her head. "Is this truck yours?"

Sexy Guy placed a protective hand on his daughter's slight shoulder. "Luce, watch your manners."

The man making her heart beat like it was in the middle of an

Olympic triathlon was a dad. Probably had a wife. That might have been the little woman who'd just made her temperamental exit.

As for his daughter, the girl was precocious and spoke her mind. Alice liked that in a person, whether man or child. But Lucy wasn't the only one who could be direct. "Yes, it is. And who might you be?"

"Lucy. I'm twelve." Sharp chin elevating, reminded Alice what it was like to be young and having to face unexpected, crushing changes. The kid tilted her head toward Sexy Guy. "That's Zach, my dad."

Doing her best to ignore frowning Sexy Dad, Alice stretched out a hand to Lucy. "Nice to meet you. I'm Alice York."

Very adult-like, Lucy met her halfway, pumped once, let go, and grinned.

Alice's chest swelled with the feeling of having hit a home run. Quickly she stepped back. Making friends was okay. Getting attached to the girl's spunk wasn't.

An older man, with a striking resemblance to Zach, ambled down the porch steps to join them. He circled Duke with a low whistle before stopping next to Alice. "This your rig, young lady?"

She grinned. Young was a relative term. On some days like today, twenty-six didn't feel as young as it should. "Yes."

After introductions, he ogled Duke and the over-the-top gypsy-colored canopy nestled in the bed. When he was done, twinkling blue eyes fastened on Alice. "Beautiful. Just beautiful."

She swallowed sudden laughter. The older version of Zach had a lot more charm than his more youthful relative.

Lucy leaned into the old guy's arm. "Papa, Penelope, and

Blake are gone."

"Good riddance is all I have to say."

Zach rolled his eyes. "Granddad, I'm trying to teach her manners."

"And a good father you are, too." Granddad slapped Zach on the back. "Those two were freeloaders. I'm not sorry to see them go."

"You're impossible. You know that, right?" The fight had gone out of Zach's tone, replaced by laughter threatening to pull his fascinating mouth into a crooked smile.

Sexy Guy clearly loved his grandfather. Grudgingly she gave him another point. But just because he was racking up good-guy points didn't mean she could jump his bones the first chance she got, even though that was exactly the insane image floating through her surprisingly alert mind.

Stop staring, Alice ordered her out-of-control libido.

Sudden desire took a nosedive when he turned a stern eye in her direction. "You'll have to call a tow truck and get that—" eyes narrowed, he gestured rudely at Duke. "—moved as soon as possible. This is a no-parking zone."

Alice's hackles stood up to be counted. "We won't be here long if I can find a store that carries the part."

Zach's granddad rubbed his chin. "That truck's a classic. Won't be easy to find parts on a Friday night. And a holiday weekend to boot."

Frustration matching Zach Barret's replaced the temper she'd been holding with a tight reign. Broke down in a no-park zone in Sellwood, with no way to lay her hands on the part she needed, put a serious knot in the timeline she'd allotted to get to the new job. No job meant no money. No money meant being stuck. And unlike these nice strangers in their nice house, getting stuck in one place was the last thing she would let happen again.

Several calls later, she paced beside Duke, the cell still glued to her ear, while Lucy explored inside the caravan, and Zach and his grandfather debated the merits of Fords versus Chevys.

The bottom line was the pump wouldn't be available until Tuesday morning, at which time her wallet would get considerably lighter.

When she was done ordering the part, Zach abandoned the debate with his grandfather. "If you release the break, we can back this thing into the drive."

Thing? What the heck?

Sexy Guy didn't give her a chance to declare she didn't need his help, but opened the passenger-side door, and waited for her to get in the driver's seat. When she didn't immediately take him up on his offer, the quick stare he shot in her direction suggested his already stretched-too-thin patience was on its last leg.

Snapping her mouth shut, she climbed in, pretending she didn't notice the flex of man muscles beneath the cotton shirt, sleeves rolled up to his elbows, as he put his shoulder to the jam and pushed.

"Granddad, give us a hand, would you? Miss York? Break?"

Swallowing the hitch of breathtaking up residence in her throat, she released the break. John and Lucy pushed from the front. Zach put his impressive muscles to work, robbing her of coherent thought for a bit too long. At the last minute, she remembered to turn the wheel so Duke would angle into the drive.

Stumbling from the cab, she hoped Zach hadn't noticed how much he'd unsettled her usual calm, take-the-road-of-least-resistance approach to life. Lucy grabbed her hand, and despite her protests, Alice found herself across the roomy kitchen table from the impetuous girl, while Zach grilled ham and cheese sandwiches at the stove.

It was John's, "You have to eat. You may as well eat with us," that tempted her.

"My dad's a great cook," Lucy had weighed in.

Against her better judgment, Alice lost the argument to keep her distance. It was Zach's pinched expression at the invitation that finally convinced her to take his grandfather up on the offer.

Deep down where she let no one see, she wondered what it was about this man, of the few she'd met in her travels, that made her aware of things she didn't want to feel again.

For her piece of mind, she needed to stay far away from Sexy Guy and his charming family. Nothing good would come of getting chummy with this hot stranger.

"Do you sleep in the caravan?" The girl's curiosity was endless.

"Sometimes."

"Sweet!"

Zach put plates of golden sandwiches and sliced apples in the middle of the table. "Go wash your hands, Luce. And while you're back there, tell Granddad dinner's on the table."

Sexy Guy stayed where he was for a long minute after his daughter left, making Alice's nerves tingle – in a good way, dang it. "Can I…um…set the table or something?"

"I'm sorry I was rude earlier." The apology came out slowly in an attention-grabbing baritone, layered with just the right amount of regret. "I have a hard time keeping staff."

Alice's stomach did a funny little somersault.

Unable to sit still under his sheepish gaze, she headed for

the cupboards looking for plates and napkins. The kitchen sparkled. Through the archway, the living area was neat as a pin. Men didn't usually live that way, and neither did pre-teen girls. "You have staff?"

"We have four residents, including my granddad, living here at Martha's Elder House. Penelope managed the house. Blake was our driver and handyman."

"And John and Lucy didn't like them." An easy assumption.

"Where are you planning to stay tonight?" he asked at the same time, putting the table between them.

Alice was glad for the subconscious message. She didn't want to be tempted. Married once, with what she thought was a bright future ahead of them, she'd learned her lesson the hard way As appealing as it might be to hang around long enough to get to know the handsome single dad, she didn't need any reason to stay in Sellwood once she'd replaced Duke's fuel pump.

She sighed regretfully. They were two ships passing in the night. Too bad. Still, her traitorous pulse pounded out a beat like a high school cheerleader. *Zach, Zach, he's our man...*

"Caravan." The word came out sharper than she intended. Sexy Guy watched her, curiosity changing his expression into something much more diverting. She softened her tone. "I'll stay in the caravan."

His granddad, John, he'd introduced himself, came into the kitchen with Lucy right behind him. "No, you won't. With Penelope and Blake gone, we have two empty rooms in the basement. You can stay in one of them until your truck is fixed."

She shook her head. "I don't want to put you out—" Or stay too long under the same roof with the family that belonged to Sexy Guy.

John shot a pointed look at Zach. That couldn't be good.

9

"You're not putting us out, is she, Zach?"

Looking uncomfortable, Zach shrugged. "No. Of course, you're not."

Lucy grabbed her hand. "Stay with us. Dad, tell her she has to stay."

"You're welcome to stay," he obliged his daughter, eyes twinkling briefly as though enjoying a private joke at Alice's expense.

Dang it. Grace under fire. Another point in his good guy tally.

Lucy let go of Alice and shoved her hands in her pants pockets. "We would like it if you'd stay."

We? She highly doubted that. And where had the girl learned to negotiate like a sixteen-year-old in a twelve-year-old's body?

"Lucy, sit down and eat your dinner, and leave Ms. York alone. She'll stay if she wants." The unapologetic mischief was gone. Zach scrubbed the counter by the stove as though he'd made a huge mess while making dinner.

Alice *wished* things could be different. "I can't. Really."

Zach stopped scrubbing, his intense gaze landing on her face. He still looked rattled, but he said gruffly, "You can."

Oh, good grief. At least now she knew where his daughter got her powers of persuasion.

Alice gave in. Reluctantly. She couldn't fight all three of them.

"Thanks for the offer." *Push and shove was more like it.* "I'll stay. But only until Tuesday or Wednesday when I get Duke going again."

Chapter 2

C haffing at his predicament, Zach ate his sandwich in silence and listened to his daughter talk excitedly with the woman whose painfully bright truck was parked at Martha's curbside. He didn't have time for the kink Penelope's temperamental departure had put in the peaceful order he'd worked hard to establish.

The growing list of orders that waited for his attention would take up every second he wasn't spending with Lucy over the long weekend. Sleep was going to be a dangling carrot on the distant horizon.

His daughter giggled.

Lucy was not a giggler. Nor did she usually speak to strangers. So what was it about Alice York that brought out the kid in his usually serious child?

Not the same thing that had given him a wallop at their first meeting on that rare, sunny spring day, he was sure. One minute he was chasing after the humorless Penelope, an act of desperation really, and the next he'd been struck by a bolt of lightning in the guise of a bright, flowing, red-flowered dress clinging to long legs and a rounded bottom.

The owner of that bottom had been swallowed by the engine compartment of a truck that was so old that no one remembered the early models anymore. Or just a few select enthusiasts anyway.

His mouth had gone dry at the trim ankles visible between black leggings and old-fashioned red sneakers, it'd been a full minute before he could swallow. What could he say? He was an ankle man when he took the time to notice the opposite sex. Which wasn't often.

Selling Japanese golf clubs online paid the bills. Taking care of Lucy and making sure Martha's Elder House functioned without any hiccups ate up the rest of his time.

"Lucy, clear the table please." His daughter made a face, but she took the plates to the sink.

Zach turned his attention to Alice. Unfortunately, he hadn't put his best foot forward when he'd first encountered the beautiful owner of the Ford. "Where were you headed when your fuel pump gave out?"

"Longview, Washington. I've got a job there."

"What kind of job, if you don't mind me asking?"

"I don't mind." She nestled her chin in the palm of her hand, the sparkle in her eyes snapping with wry humor. "I work on classic cars."

Remembering his first sight of her, he asked, "You're a mechanic?"

"Does that surprise you?"

The subtle scent of vanilla coming from her side of the table sent rational thought on a long hike in the opposite direction from practical reason. It was a good thing he was a grown man who had the power to stand up to steamy distractions.

"No." The stranger his granddad and Lucy had invited to stay in their basement, who said she slept in her truck when it broke down, could be anything from a burglar to a most wanted criminal.

Stunning green eyes studied him. The punch to his gut wasn't that unpleasant.

Everything about the woman, the cut of her short, wispy, strawberry-blonde hair, the flowery dress that snuggled close to curves he couldn't help noticing, and the energetic wave of slender hands when she talked with Lucy, all suggested an impulsive pixie who liked rocking the boat. He didn't like his boat rocked.

Zach drew his brows together and wished Alice York was his only problem. Finding replacements for Penelope and Blake trumped his temporary visitor. This was the second time since the first of the year that he'd had to hire staff because his crazy family had chased them off. And it wasn't even June yet.

Since his grandfather was the ringleader, it only seemed fair the old coot should be involved in coming up with a solution to fix their staffing shortage. "Granddad, what do you suggest I do about replacing Penelope and Blake?"

"Call that fancy company you use." His granddad angled a satisfied look in Zach's direction. "Though I must say, it doesn't seem like they employ the right caliber of people. Don't seem to stay around long, do they?"

Zach plastered a smile on his face. "They're closed for the holiday."

Portland Staffing Services took their three-day weekends seriously. And thanks to his granddad, who was nodding sagely as though he'd had nothing to do with Penelope and Blake's ill-timed departure, *Zach* had been promoted to sole caretaker for the four octogenarians who called Martha's home.

He had no time to be chief cook, housekeeper, driver, mechanic, dad, *and* to fill the largest orders for golf clubs he'd had since starting up the business when his grandmother passed away. Even with three of the residents away visiting family for the long weekend, the place was too much for one person to handle.

A suspicious sound came from Alice's direction. Did she find his predicament amusing?

She seemed like a woman who could do anything she set her mind to. Fixing broken trucks. Fooling a defenseless family into believing she was a normal girl wandering from one mechanic job to another. From his point of view and the way his pulse lept, there was nothing normal about the lady. In her defense though, she probably wasn't a thief or mass murderer either. There was no way she'd ever be able to skulk around in that truck.

"Not from around here?"

"No. I grew up in a military family. Moving around is in my blood."

That would explain the Marine decals on the back of her canopy. He understood military life. He'd grown up there himself. But the life of constant moving had the opposite effect on him. As soon as he could, he'd put down roots. One's that couldn't be dug up.

So she was a distraction who would move along when the next restless whim hit, not one of his new, cleverly improved weighted golf clubs that could hit a ball so far down the fairway you couldn't see where it landed. More a curiosity. A psychedelic novelty ball instead of a simple white one.

"You won't be staying long then," he stated the obvious to be sure.

"You can count on it. Like I said. Here only long enough to fix Duke."

Excellent! "I'll show you to your room."

"First let me help Lucy with the dishes." She gathered the glasses from the table so she was carrying three locked between those long-fingered hands. Graceful. Not hands he would associate with a mechanic who worked on big engines.

Lucy swung back to the table. Alice, compelling gaze still on him, making him warm up from the inside out, headed for the sink. In the middle, they collided. It happened so fast, it was like being at the circus. Water and orange juice spattered all over, including down the front of Alice's pretty dress. Glasses shattered at their feet.

Alice grabbed Lucy's arm to keep his daughter from stepping on the shards. They were both barefoot.

"Don't move, either one of you," he ordered, grabbing the broom and dustpan from the pantry, making quick work of sweeping up the dangerous pieces.

Wiping down the front of Alice's dress wouldn't be a good idea, so he sponged the floor instead, ending by wiping juice and water from the girls' feet.

Lucy was ticklish. So was his new house guest. Over his head, it started with short giggly bursts as he picked up one foot, then the next. First Lucy, then Alice. Seconds later, their laughter contagious, both lost it, leaning into each other, hands slapped over their mouths, and when he looked up, tears ran down their cheeks.

The unexpected happy sound settled in his chest, a flitting hummingbird coming to rest on a branch of his heart.

Fighting a grin teetering on the edge of joining the laughter, Zach carefully folded the kitchen towel and left it on the edge of the sink.

"Are you laughing at me?" he asked Alice softly. It wouldn't be smart to lose himself in the forest-green eyes drenched in playful amusement. Who was this woman? The no-nonsense mechanic? Or this bewitching wide-eyed, free spirit?

No sir, not stepping onto *that* slippery slope.

Instead, letting his heart turn to mush for his daughter, he watched Lucy, still giggling, disappear down the hall that led to the bathroom. Seconds later shower water could be heard hitting the tub.

"No, of course not." Alice's lingering amusement turned soft with amazement as if she'd looked inside him and seen how much he loved his daughter. She inched a step back. "You wouldn't have a second shower, would you?"

How proud he was of his daughter wasn't something he hid, since it'd always been important Lucy knew how important she was to his life. For sure, more important than any woman he might find interesting. And one reason for his still single status.

Breaking free of Alice's wistful expression was harder than it should have been. He cleared his throat. "Sure. Downstairs. Let me show you."

He led the way to the basement half convincing himself it was only sympathy he felt for the gypsy nomad, nothing more. She had no family that she mentioned. The life she lived seemed a lonely one.

"Lucy's adorable."

This from the woman who could be his daughter's doppelganger in the adorable department.

"Thanks." He showed her the bathroom and bedrooms. His

granddad had already been in, stripped, and remade the beds. "They're both empty, so you can have your pick."

In the tight quarters of the hallway, their shoulders touched. He banged against the wall in an attempt to escape the snap of attraction that sizzled to his fingertips, then cursed under his breath because Alice saw and went unnaturally still.

Guarded, she said, "I'll...um...get my things from the truck. It's been a long day."

After she'd disappeared out the front door, the truth settled in with little fanfare. Try as he might, he couldn't seem to ignore Alice York. He'd only known the woman for a day, but already discovered she was funny, imaginative, and easy on the senses.

It was hard to breathe when he got too close. He wanted to know more, but moving into a stranger's home, even temporarily, also meant she was rash, and a little too trusting. Something *he* hadn't been since Janet had told him she didn't want to be a mother to their daughter.

Completely and utterly intrigued, Zach retreated up the stairs to his office, where he stopped at the window overlooking the front of Martha's. He watched, sorting through the surprising emotions badgering him as Alice climbed into the tall, colorful canopy on the back of the truck.

The real truth was that he didn't know if he wanted to find out where this unexpected interest in his house guest would lead him. Or what it would do to the even keel of the life he'd made for himself and Lucy, which he barely held together as it was.

By the time the sun made an early appearance the next morning, he'd been up for hours burying himself in pending orders. And he'd come up with a plan. All he needed was his famous French toast—at least it was famous with his daughter and granddad—and Alice's cooperation.

When the girls wandered into the kitchen, he had place settings ready, apple juice on the table—no more orange juice for the time being—and cinnamon-covered French toast piled a mile high. Homemade maple syrup filled his grandmother's gravy dish. When he turned around to deliver the bowl to the table, the treasured memento nearly slipped from his fingers.

Rumpled from sleep in satiny pajamas the color of her eyes, Alice slumped into a chair at the table. She took a delicate, appreciative sniff. "Something smells delicious."

You look delicious.

When she glanced up and saw him staring, she straightened. Finger combing her hair only managed to cause more disarray than order, reawakening the attraction he'd taken great pains to quash with work.

His stomach clenched in distracting appreciation. The night before, his imagination shooting to the moon, it'd been almost impossible to clear the images heating him up that came with the sound of shower water splattering against the tile.

Zach forcefully reigned in the desire to reach out and touch unruly, silky strands of her strawberry-gilded hair. No way would she agree to his proposal if she thought he was an eager hound dog. Which he wasn't, despite his physician's reaction.

"Dad, can I go over to Tiffany's? Her mom said we could sell lemonade in front of her house today. Carla's going to be there, too."

Tiffany lived two doors down with her parents and little brother; Carla was across the street with her family. The three girls did everything together.

"Sure. *After* you eat breakfast."

Holding him to his word, she was finished and out the door,

before he could count to twenty, leaving him alone with Alice. Which was what he wanted, right?

His granddad's, *"Don't chase that girl away,"* when he'd left earlier for his usual Saturday morning coffee with the guys repeated like a chant in his mind. The old man's sentiment was surprising given he'd chased off everyone Zach had hired over the past year.

"How much do you make doing mechanic work?"

That swung her guarded gaze in his direction. "Enough to get me to the next place."

"Do you take on side jobs?"

The fork stopped midway to her mouth. Suspicion stiffened her jaw. "Depends. You have a car that needs work?"

Zach took a deep breath. "My grandmother died a year and a half ago. Her kidneys gave out. Granddad took it pretty hard. They'd been married fifty-five years. I thought I was going to lose him, so I bought this house, renovated it, and opened Martha's Elder House. Three of his friends moved in too."

"Where are they?"

"Spending the holiday with their families. Yesterday you saw what happens when Granddad doesn't take to the staff I hire. He likes you." He threw in for good measure, "So does Lucy."

She couldn't leave before Tuesday, but for some crazy reason, in the early hours of the morning when he was trying to convince himself he didn't need another *girl* in his life, Alice had stuck. But *that* would remain his secret.

His plan was win-win. He needed someone to help him keep Martha's going until he could hire new staff. She needed a place to stay while she waited to fix her truck.

"I'm not sure I understand." She put the fork down. "Are you offering a job?"

"Even though it's just the three of us for the weekend, Martha's doesn't run smoothly without help. The van needs work. I have a business to run. Someone has to keep an eye on the place while I fill orders. I'm hoping you'll be interested in taking the job."

"I have to be at my next job by the end of the week."

"I'll take whatever time you can give. You have to wait for your truck part, right? Longview is only an hour's drive from here, so you could get there in no time at all."

"I'd have to leave by Thursday night at the latest."

"Like I said, I'll take whatever you can give me." He didn't mean that the way it sounded, but couldn't take the words back when her forest-green eyes grew dark and inscrutable.

Alice pushed feathery bangs off her face, exposing her uncertainty.

Was she nervous about making even a temporary commitment? Or was it just him that made her shift uneasily in her chair? If it was, Zach sympathized. He didn't need her pushing his pulse into the stratosphere.

He should let her leave, and try to manage on his own until he could get someone else, but he knew he couldn't. He needed the money the new orders would bring to Martha's.

"I don't know. I have to think about it," she said, the words little more than a croak.

Chapter 3

Alice studied the man dangling an opportunity to make money. On the surface, his offer seemed innocent enough. And with her extra-light wallet, it was a godsend. But she knew danger when she saw it disguised as six feet of sizzling hot, hunky male. Short, thick, light-brown hair had seen a comb that morning, though apparently wasn't interested in lying down. Blue eyes made her think of the depths of Crater Lake in Central Oregon. Serene. More hidden beneath the surface than reflected above.

Not secrets exactly. But, the real man? Who was he?

It didn't matter. It was clear he had roots growing to China, which made him the kind of man Alice avoided at all costs. Men who would want her to give up the road, had her running for the hills.

But Zach Barret loved his daughter and grandfather, his family. If she wasn't careful, he could have her reexamining the life she'd chosen. Being near him and the steady gaze that seemed to see straight into her heart, heating her up in ways she'd never been heated, not even with her ex, was like walking into a fairy-tale romance she could buy off the internet or bookshelf.

She'd already tried the fairy tale and failed miserably.

Still, there was no denying he would tempt any woman determined to stay single and live life her way. He made her breathless. And question why she couldn't linger, maybe get to know the little burg of Sellwood better. Yup, he was dangerous. With a capital D.

She should go. Immediately. Except she couldn't.

His eyes took on a calculating glint, a warning he wasn't planning to play fair. "I'll give you room and board, and a week's wage."

A week's wage. Inside Alice groaned. She could use the money. Her palms turned clammy. That she was imagining the man waiting for an answer to his enticing offer as more than an employer, and a temporary one at that, put the fear of...well, god...into her.

He had a daughter and grandfather he'd built his life around. He was responsible. Dependable. Practical. All things she had no experience in dealing with men, except her grandpa.

He tempted her, dang it! To stay and explore all the facets that made up Zach Barret, including what it would be like to investigate the solid physique keeping her on the edge of wanting to reach out and touch.

Oh no you don't. Alice took a mental step back.

His job offer was a temporary gig. And Zach Barret was just another employer in a long line of jobs that allowed her to be on her way. "I'll stay until I have to leave for Longview."

The corners of his eyes crinkled. "Good."

Her decision made, Alice took her plate to the sink. "Where

do you want me to start?"

For a second, a look flashed in his eyes that had her forgetting her vow to step away from the man. Then the spark was gone and he was the boss, owner of Martha's. "I have work to do in the office. If you would check out the van and make sure it's in good running condition, that would be great."

"I'll clean the kitchen first."

He disappeared upstairs without comment, making her wonder if she'd really seen that momentary heat darkening the blue of his eyes.

Don't play this game. You know how badly it ends.

Alice dispensed with the dirty dishes, allowing memories to emerge she rarely took time to examine. They were old news for sure, water under the bridge and all that. Her parents divorce when she was thirteen. Going to live with her beloved grandfather because neither parent wanted to be bothered with raising an angry, confused teenager. Thinking she'd found true love, her misguided wedding at eighteen to her high school boyfriend.

She'd been young and too naive.

Her grandfather had tried to tell her, and she'd sworn to him her marriage wouldn't end like her parents. Then one day she was holding divorce papers because of course, it hadn't been love after all. Not on his part. And not hers, she'd finally accepted years later.

Marriage wasn't in her playbook. And she'd added another rule since. Despite how much she was tempted, no sex with single dads, or men with roots buried so deep it would take a bulldozer to dig them out.

Swiping the counter dry, and marveling at how much she'd *liked* cleaning Zach's kitchen, Alice hung the towel on the oven door and went to change into her work clothes. Putting all thoughts behind her of how much fun it would be to get to know him in the biblical sense, she went to do something productive— like check out the van in the garage.

Chapter 4

To clear his head, not from the work—that was easy stuff—but from his absorbed preoccupation with the woman he'd hired to be his temporary help, Zach went downstairs. Alice was a beautiful and interesting lady, but he'd better get himself under control before he did something he would regret, like letting his attraction for the rambling rose grow into something more when it was clear the sentiment wasn't returned.

Grabbing a cola, he headed to the backyard. Rare, sunny days in a string of rainy weeks that in most years didn't let up until June didn't come often. Settling on the bench to do some heavy thinking, he took a long swing of his drink. Tugging at the collar of his shirt, he fumbled to unbutton the top button.

The lush gardens, Buck and Betty's pride and joy should have brought calm to his inconvenient desire to get to know the real Alice York shielded beneath the pretty face she presented to the world. Finding himself wanting her in his bed too, was not good timing on his part. Alice had made it very clear. She had no intention of staying any longer than the six days he'd hired her for. So it was settled. She was his employee. Nothing more. Never would be. He could put all this messy attraction behind him and get back to work.

Pleased to have that problem solved, Zach finished his cola.

A sudden clunk came from the garage followed by a woman's eloquent curse. The graphic expletive layered with pain launched Zach to his feet. Bursting into the smaller building painted the same slate gray as the house, he found Alice scooting from under the van perched up on car ramps.

If his heart wasn't pounding so hard, he would have smiled. A sailor had nothing on her creative vocabulary. Waiting until her head cleared the metal of the vehicle, he gripped her elbow and hauled the trying woman to her feet. "What happened? Are you all right?"

She cradled her hand. Blood oozed from her knuckles. "It's nothing serious. Just banged my hand on the transmission trying to get the oil pan off."

He stated the obvious. "You're bleeding."

Her wary gaze darted to his. "There's blood because the da… ng bolt was stuck and when it finally broke loose— I scrape my knuckles all the time."

"I'll take you to urgent care. You need a tetanus shot."

"Had one last year. No urgent care," Alice said, her jaw taking on stubborn like it was a natural fit. She dabbed at her hand with a clean shop rag.

Zach winced. "At least come in the house and let me bandage those knuckles."

"Don't be such a girl." Her teasing smile demolished his decision to play it cool. He was back at square one, crushing on a girl who would never fit into his life.

Chapter 4

Because his heart was still beating hard, he didn't give Alice a choice but marched her cute little ass to the kitchen where he had a first aid kit.

"I'll clean it with soap, then put iodine antiseptic on it." Living in a house with a twelve-year-old and four octogenarians had made him an expert at taking care of small surface wounds.

He gently nudged her hand under cold water, carefully washing the blood away. It was Alice's turn to wince. It obviously wasn't the first time she'd had scrapes treated. She leaned into his arm, her subtle vanilla scent making him a little dizzy, and suddenly wanting to explore the pulse points where the distracting smell would have its greatest potency.

Chin resting on his shoulder, her soft curves took his mind far from the first aid he was rendering. His breath hitched in his throat. If he turned just the tiniest bit to face her, she would know exactly how much her nearness affected him.

He angled slightly in the opposite direction, ordering himself to pay attention to the task at hand and not Alice, who was bringing his blood to a sizzling boil.

By the time he had the wound cleaned and the worst of her scrapes covered in bandages, all he could think about was stealing a kiss. Just a quick one. To see if she tasted as good as she smelled. And so he could ease the hardness in his body, a need he hadn't attended to in a long time.

Her hand trembled. He quickly looked at her face. Alice wouldn't meet his gaze. Her cheeks flushed a bright red. Because she felt the attraction flaring between them?

Chucking caution out the back door, he watched, fascinated by the battle between desire and not-going-to-go-there playing across the face that would stop any man passing her on the street in his tracks. Unable to resist, he tilted her chin and lowered his mouth to hers.

Her surprised intake of breath and soft, *oh,* drew him in deeper than Zach intended. Alice flattening her hands on his chest and leaning into the kiss sent every rational, sane thought on a triathlon into the wilderness. She tasted...sweet, and felt...like she belonged in his arms, and because his world had taken a disorienting wobble to the right, he lost his head.

The kitchen door banged behind him. "Dad, do we have any sugar? Tiffany's mom ran out and we need more."

He jumped back, nearly knocking Alice off her feet. He steadied her with one hand on her shoulder but from a safe distance. It would be too easy to cross that electrified space and take up where they'd left off at his daughter's interruption.

He faced Lucy. "There's a full bag in the pantry."

Lucy's mouth hung open. She snapped it shut. "Were you guys kissing?"

"No! Of course not," he blurted.

Beside him, Alice snorted.

His heart beat a frantic rhythm, but now for a different reason. What did his twelve-year-old know about kissing?

Abruptly Lucy disappeared into the walk-in. From inside her voice drifted out. "Well. You should keep kissing."

She came out wearing a crooked grin and was gone with the bag of sugar before Zach could stop sputtering enough to formulate a logical, adult response that would go something like, no,...they wouldn't keep kissing. He'd lost his mind for a minute. It would not happen again.

He should apologize. Squaring his shoulders to do just that, he found Alice covering her mouth with her uninjured hand, shoulders shaking.

"Not funny," he told her. "Lucy shouldn't know anything

about kissing, much less be advising her father to keep doing it!"

"She's twelve. She knows about kissing."

"She's my little girl. There will be no kissing until she's thirty. And maybe not even then."

"You should have seen the look on your face." Eyes crinkled with barely contained laughter softened. "You're a good dad."

Zach crossed his arms to keep from reaching for the woman to continue where they'd left off. "What look?"

"Like a daddy deer caught in headlights."

"I was…mortified actually," Zach admitted now that he was looking back from a safe distance.

Delicate brows shot up.

"Not about the kissing part," he stammered. When the humor twitching her mouth threatened to spill out again, he resolutely trudged forward. "I don't usually kiss women in front of my daughter."

Cocking a hip, Alice leaned against the counter. She was enjoying his discomfort a little too much. "Usually?"

"Never. I never kiss women in front of Lucy." Realizing he was again alone in the house with the very delectable Alice York, in desperation he searched for a safe distraction. "How about taking a walk to get some coffee? The Coffee House is not far. And you'd get to see a bit of Sellwood on the way."

"What about your work?"

"I could use a break." A walkabout town would clear his head of the image of Alice melting in his arms.

As if she could read his mind, the humor drained from her face."Sure. Me, too. Give me five minutes to change my clothes."

While he waited, fighting the fact that he was looking forward to spending what was left of the morning with the woman disrupting his balanced routine, Zach put the first aid kit back in the cupboard. What the heck had gotten into him?

When Alice returned in exactly six minutes—not that he was counting—he held the back door open for her. To prove to himself what he already knew, he had to ask, "Do you ever dream of staying in one place for more than a week or two?"

Chapter 5

"I'm living my dream, " Alice told Zach firmly. A chill supplanted her earlier desire to see where a simple kiss could take them. She should have known nothing about Zach Barret was simple. "And I enjoy traveling, seeing new places, living the American dream."

It was better than getting trapped in a loveless marriage like her parents. Better than bringing a kid that wasn't wanted into that marriage. And then repeating their mistake. That was the worst.

Zach stared thoughtfully at her for a long moment. "That's not the American dream."

"Sure it is." She didn't know what it was about him that had her wanting to push his buttons. Maybe it was because he was so dang serious. And cute. "I'm exploring a better life and loving it."

"Perhaps. But don't you get lonely moving from place to place?"

Lonely? Of course not.

The welcome she'd found in the many towns she'd visited since leaving her grandpa's place was so much better than her childhood. Now that had been a lonely existence.

"I meet a lot of interesting people—" She was ready to give him a whole list of reasons why she loved the life she'd chosen, and why she wouldn't give in to the enticement of hanging around to get to know an incredibly hot guy who was bravely raising his daughter all alone. But they'd stopped at Lucy and her friend's lemonade stand, effectively ending her attempt to explain her choices.

She didn't owe anyone an explanation anyway.

Zach handed her a paper cup filled to the brim with the sweetly tart drink and paid the girls. "I'll just be a second. Need to tell Tiffany's mom where we're going. She's on kid-watching duty today. Luce, introduce your friends to Alice."

When he left her with the girls, Alice found herself unexpectedly tongue-tied. Twelve had not been a good year for her. A military brat who moved frequently, she'd never mastered the art of making friends as these three had.

Lucy did as she was told and introduced her friends—Carla, brown-skinned, with flashing dimples and sparkling brown eyes, and Tiffany whose coloring was close enough to Lucy's blonde hair and blue eyes to be mistaken for her sister—before pointing in the direction of Duke. "That's Alice's truck. Isn't it sweet? Sometimes she sleeps in it!"

"Can we see?" Carla bounced up on her tiptoes.

"Sure." Alice followed the chattering girls, gulping enough lemonade so it wouldn't spill on the way. Unlocking the caravan-style door, she stood back to watch.

The girls and their oohs and awes struck a chord of envy in Alice's chest. She'd had one friend when she was twelve. Arlita.

Arlita's family was from Hawaii. They met at school at Camp Pendleton when both families were stationed there. Military kids were used to moving on, so when Alice had been sent to live with her grandpa at the same time that Arlita's family went to the islands, their letters had crossed the ocean but hadn't lasted long.

Lucy was lucky.

Rare longing pummeled Alice. She forced her fingers to relax around the keys to her truck. She was happy with Duke being her only friend these days. Really. She was.

"What's this," Tiffany asked.

"The bed. Unhook the latch and you'll see."

The three girls giggled. Lucy released the latch, carefully lowering the cot Alice had installed.

They crawled onto the bed chattering like magpies. The happy sound cracked the barriers Alice had erected over the years. She chewed on the inside of her cheek. *Was she lonely?* Maybe once in a while, but not often enough to let the pinch of it last. At least she hadn't thought so since taking to the road.

"Ready?"

Zach's voice at her elbow sent goosebumps of awareness skittering up her spine. Pasting a smile on her face, she faced the man inspiring second thoughts about the future she'd chosen. "Sure."

Zach helped the girls down from the back of Duke. Herding them like a mother hen gathering his chicks, he sent them back to their lemonade stand with firm instructions, "Be good for Mrs. Garrison."

Alice's father had never taken that much interest in what she was doing. Yup. Lucy was one lucky girl.

The sun came out from behind a cloud. A sense of weightlessness spread through Alice's chest as she stared at Zach, thinking about all the masks he wore. Businessman. Entrepreneur. Grandson. Father. Protector of the elderly and innocent children. Could he also be a friend, too? He would be her first in a long time.

Comfortable silence accompanied them for the first block as they walked toward the business district of Sellwood. It was nice, but she was too curious about the man shortening his stride to match hers, even as worry niggled and got in line in front of the curiosity. "Kid duty? Are the girls safe out by the road like that?"

He sent her a surprised glance.

"Sure. It's a quiet neighborhood. And we keep a very close eye on them, taking turns, so one of us knows where they are at all times."

"They're sweet girls." Alice didn't want to explain her concern. It wasn't something she talked about.

"We think so." He waited a beat for her to offer more. When she didn't, he said, "It's good for Lucy to spend time with the other girls. She has some separation anxiety because of her mother taking off, so I've been trying to teach her to be a little bit independent."

She and Lucy had a lot in common, only Alice had learned to be independent the hard way. If she'd had a dad who cared as much as Zach did, things might have turned out differently. "She'll appreciate that when she's older."

"I hope so." He shoved his hands in the pockets of his jeans. "Sundays we keep for family time."

Family time. There was a foreign concept. But the pinch that came with it wasn't foreign. Tomorrow was Sunday. It would be another day she would be an outsider looking in.

Clasping her hands behind her back, she added a bounce to her step she hoped matched the excitement she pretended. It ended up not being all pretend. "So tell me about Sellwood."

She loved exploring new places. And to do it with a good-looking guy? Well, it was kind of nice for a change. "Where are we going for coffee?"

"I guess that depends on what kind of coffee you want."

What followed was a lively debate over what constituted the best cup of joe. To her amazement, Alice enjoyed their banter more than she should.

While giving her an interesting history of Sellwood as they went, Zach led them to a quaint coffee shop in the heart of the little community's antique row called The Java Roasters.

Alice liked her coffee black with just a touch of cream and sugar. After a cautious sip, she had to admit her companion was right. "Okay. You win. This *is* the perfect cup of coffee."

Amusement reached deep into blue eyes and made them sparkle as he held the door open so they could resume their walking tour. "Don't sound so disappointed."

She couldn't resist the seductive invitation to flirt with Zach. Taking a deep breath of spring air, eyes locked on his, she said playfully, "I've read somewhere, it's the little treasures that make life so interesting."

Grinning, brows arching, he let the door close behind them. "If you like *treasures*, you'll love this little antique store on the next block. Gram's Treasures. My grandmother loved going there."

They stopped at the next corner waiting for the light to change, the air between them suddenly simmering with tension. A renegade shiver hopscotched up her spine. The busy Saturday street traffic faded. Her heart thumped. His masculine scent wrapped around her, pulling Alice inexplicably closer, making her pulse leap and her imagination take flight.

Out of nowhere, his strong arm slid around her shoulders. She leaned into his firm chest. His lips covered hers. Alice melted into a happy puddle at the sound, feel, and taste of Zach Barret – hard muscles beneath his shirt, lingering coffee mixed with heady man, the low growl at the back of his throat.

Alice let go and dove in over her head. Losing track of where they were, she let Zach in, reveled in how he explored her mouth and crushed her to his chest, his fists bunching in her dress at the small of her back. And she didn't want to quit. Didn't want to squander the promise for more his kiss gave.

Finally, a long wolf whistle broke them apart. Alice's face burned.

Zach grabbed her arm, pulling her across the intersection into a shady window alcove in a newer brick building housing the library. He warned her, "I don't do one-night stands."

Alice swallowed hard. "Neither do I."

"No more kissing."

"No more kissing," she sadly agreed, mourning the loss.

Too bad. He was a great kisser. Maybe the best she'd ever experienced. Not that she'd kissed many men. But he was right. No point in starting something she didn't plan to finish.

He dropped her arm. "Gram's Treasures is at the end of this block."

She drew back her shoulders to put as much space between them as possible. If he could act like their kiss meant nothing, so could she. She briefly touched her lips. She swallowed. Really, she could.

"Oh, hell," he mumbled as he lowered his face to hers. Her determination to hang on to a responsible distance melted into squishy gelatin.

But someone had to take charge. *Enough.* She wedged her hands between them and pushed.

He lifted his head, his breath coming fast. "This isn't working."

"Yes, it is." Alice stepped around him careful not to brush against the man calling her like an alpha wolf would his playmate.

"Let's check out that fabled antique store," she said, heading toward the note-worthy shop. When she left for Longview she didn't want to leave anything behind. Especially not her heart!

Too damned attracted to the man, and acutely aware he stretched his long legs to catch up, she marched up to the last shop in the long building. A placard hung over the door proclaiming it Gram's Treasures.

She would not. Not. End up in a relationship that had the remotest possibility of ending in a cold divorce like her parents. Not that he'd asked her on a date, much less for anything more permanent. Whatever the sudden excitement was growing in her belly, she had to nip it in the bud. "They're closed."

Zach leaned over her shoulder, staring at the sign hanging in the windowed door. "Not possible. Gram's is never closed."

"Guess there's a first time for everything," she said, stumbling over the words, then wished she didn't sound like a complete bonehead who'd never been kissed by the best-looking guy on the block.

He crossed the street with her. Alice ducked into the nearest door, determined to shake off, if not the man, then at least the churning in her stomach. She could like Zach. Maybe even more than like him. Which wasn't smart. She'd only known the man for barely twenty-four hours.

When he didn't crowd her as she sought to lose herself

among the multitude of treasures from the past, Alice's nerves gradually settled. He disappeared up one aisle, while she went in the opposite direction at the next intersection of overflowing passages. Finally, she was able to breathe easy.

"Tomorrow's Sunday." Zach's deep voice made her jump, her hand knocking a cut-glass sugar bowl off a nearby self.

She scrambled to catch it, but he was quicker, saving the bowl before it splintered on the floor. He carefully placed it back on the shelf, and it was then Alice realized what a quagmire she'd fallen into. If he handled a woman with as much care–

What was she thinking? Did she, for the first time in seven years, want to give up the road and permanently park Duke?

"That was clumsy of me." she sputtered, stunned at the direction her thoughts had taken. "Thanks."

Concern turned his blue eyes dark. "I'm taking Granddad and Lucy to Oaks Park tomorrow. You want to go with us?"

"Why?"

"Why not? You don't have anyone else expecting you to show up on a Sunday afternoon, do you?"

And there was the crux of her life. Yup, she was *definitely* in deep doggy do-do.

~ * ~

Alice stared at the painting sitting on the easel she'd set up in the small space of her caravan after returning from her walk with Zach. Late afternoon light filtered through the high windows she'd had built into the frame of the canopy, casting a soft glow on the merry-go-round that was the focal point of the painting.

Zach's kiss lingered on her lips. Kissing him had been a monumental mistake she couldn't shake off. But worse, his invitation to join his family on the one day reserved for family time was...

She dabbed paint on the canvas.

...Confusing...

She dabbed more paint, darker gray this time, and stood back. Something was missing.

...And his kiss oh-my-god...disturbing...

Definitely disturbing. Why would he want a stranger to spend time with the family he loved more than anything else? And how could she turn down an opportunity to spend a day with a family who knew how to do it right? Unlike hers, who'd had it all wrong from day one.

She understood part of her attraction to Zach was how dedicated he was to Lucy and his granddad. As far as she could tell, he would never consider walking away and making a life without them.

More paint went on the canvas, a stormy gray.

The only solution was to separate herself from any desire to be a part of the community he'd made inside Martha's Elder House. She'd tried and failed to make the family she'd desperately wanted after her parents left her at her grandpa's. With George, who'd given up on her after she lost their baby so late in her pregnancy. The doctors said it wasn't her fault, but she'd never been able to believe them.

Shortly after, her widowed grandfather had remarried. He'd wanted her to stay with him and his new wife, but she'd known there was no place in his life for her anymore, and so she'd hit the road.

A soft knock snapped her back to the present.

"Dinner's ready." Zach's steady, sexy baritone had her doing the unthinkable—wishing for what she couldn't have.

She carefully set aside her palate of colors, angling so she blocked his view of the painting. "I'm not hungry."

He climbed into her home on wheels, crowding her. Everything about Zach Barret was so large. His commanding presence. The ease with which he took care of his family. The surprised smile lighting deep blue eyes as he stared over her shoulder at the one thing she didn't want him to see. "You're a painter."

Every female molecule in her body came to attention with a low, exasperating hum. When Zach was born, God should have stamped a warning on his forehead. *Dangerous. Stay away from this man or lose your heart.*

Alice shrugged. She painted to soothe the memories but didn't share the finished canvases with anyone. Not even her grandpa. "It's a hobby."

"This one's beautiful."

Frowning, she studied the painting. What did he see in the bold strokes of a haze-covered, empty playground?

"What's wrong?" He moved closer, his chest brushing her arm, as though he wanted to protect her like he did Lucy.

The ridiculous thought surprised her. She didn't need protection.

Facing the painting, reaching with the tip of the brush, hovering before she touched the still-wet paint, she said softly, "Something's missing."

There was a long silence at her back, then, "There's no children. It's missing children playing on the merry-go-round."

Alice hung her head. Leave it to a stranger to notice the pain that never went away.

Strong arms slid around her shoulders, offering comfort she had no right to take.

There were no children in any of her paintings. And none in

Chapter 5

her life either.

Chapter 6

Zach watched Alice talk with his daughter as if the moment that had shattered his equilibrium in her caravan had never happened. His arms wrapped around her, he'd seen the canvases standing on the floor, leaning against the wall; one of a lone, sturdy maple tree with an empty tire swing hanging by ropes; another of a bedraggled, worn-around-the-edges cottage, no lights in the windows, weeds growing in the yard, nothing to welcome home the woman who'd painted the heart-wrenching pictures.

Empty of children, families, or pets of any kind, the paintings were masterful, poignant, and very revealing. They touched a place inside him with profound loneliness. If the paintings were a reflection of her heart, and her life was as empty as they were, whether she understood or not, all Alice's traveling was a search for something to fill that void.

When he'd kissed her, her response hadn't felt empty. And try as he might, he couldn't forget how perfectly she fit in his arms.

Briefly closing his eyes to clear the memory, he vowed, no more kissing.

He had Lucy. And Martha's. Sure, there were times when the rhythm of his days was routine, with no glamour, and little excitement. Certainly, they weren't filled with the same flash of excitement that had washed over him like an electric storm while he'd kissed the daylights out of Alice.

He was happy with his life. There was no future in taking a side trip into the mythical land of happy-ever-after, which he didn't believe in anyway.

Bothered that even after his pep talk, he still cared about Alice spending her days...and nights alone, he interrupted the lively conversation going on about the bikini swimsuit he hadn't allowed Lucy to buy, favoring a bright green one-piece instead. "Luce, I invited Alice to go to Oaks Park with us tomorrow. She said she'd think about it."

Lucy jumped out of her chair. "Oh! You have to come."

Alice looked at him for the first time since he'd seen her paintings, and talked her into coming to dinner, hungry or not. It hurt to think of her being alone. He was not leaving this lovely woman home while they went off to have fun at Oaks Park. He didn't know why, but it seemed like she deserved some play time of her own.

The look she gave him promised trouble. He had no problem with not playing fair. Winking, he sent her a silent message, *bring it on lady.*

Gorgeous eyes narrowing in suspicion, she stared hard at him. "I have work to finish on the van."

He arched his brows. It might be unwise, but Lucy was his ace in the hole. His daughter didn't give up easily when she wanted something bad enough. Sure enough, his scamp of a daughter leaned toward Alice. "Pleeease. I want you to come."

He could barely hold his own when his baby girl turned that pleading, innocent face in his direction. He hoped Alice couldn't fight it either. Or fight his granddad, who jumped in with, "You have to come. It's an amusement park. Been around since 1905. You'll love it."

"The park doesn't open until noon on Sundays," Zach said, holding his breath as indecision played across her pretty face. "You'll have time to work on the van in the morning."

Ignoring him, Alice tweaked Lucy's cheek. "Okay, I'll go with you. But only because you asked so nicely."

The back she presented to him gave ample warning, *back off buddy.* He was going to pay for using his family to manipulate her.

"How about we do up these dishes for your dad," Alice said. She was quiet while Lucy chattered like a magpie, enthusing about Oaks Park and its rides as she put the dishes in the dishwasher.

Shortly after, with a brief goodbye tossed in his direction, Alice went to her room.

Lucy gave him a tight hug, which he gladly returned. "Love you, Dad."

"Love you too, kiddo." Zach tugged her slight body closer, grateful he had her. For so long she'd been the only light in his life. He added his special promise, "A whole sky-full."

Lucy wiggled free. "Love you more."

Flashing a grin, she left a sweet drive-by kiss on her grandfather's cheek, leaving the men in her life to finish out the evening together; not a hardship in Zach's opinion.

He shook his head, slightly bemused, but mostly confused. Lucy never failed to amaze him. He'd loved watching her grow from a loving toddler into an incredible young girl. That wasn't the confusing part. It was his greatest pleasure.

The confusion came from realizing, for the first time since his daughter's birth, there could be another woman in his life. Another woman who didn't want to set down roots and become part of a family and community.

Like Lucy's mother, who didn't want to be a wife or mother. After she'd placed their brand new daughter in his arms, Janet had disappeared into a life that didn't include either of them. He'd wanted to try. She'd wanted to explore the world unencumbered by the two she was leaving behind. They hadn't heard from her since.

He'd read somewhere that people fell in love over and over with the same type of person. If the excitement he was feeling was anything remotely resembling love, he didn't need another Janet who wouldn't stick. It would break Lucy's heart.

Sighing, he went to the coffee pot. "Coffee, Granddad?"

His grandfather nodded, frowning.

Zach waited until the coffee finished brewing, poured a cup and placed it within easy reach on the table. "Something on your mind?"

"Our girl lives a lonely life."

At first, Zach didn't follow. His heart sputtered in sudden fear. "Lucy?"

His granddad shook his head, shooting him a look that gave nothing away. "Alice."

Our girl? Yes, she did.

Zach sat across from the older man. "I don't think she would agree."

His granddad took a thoughtful sip of his coffee. "I'm not going to be around forever. We have to make her see how much we want her to stay."

"What are you saying, Granddad?" Zach leaned over the table toward him. "You're as healthy as a horse—unless there's something you haven't told me."

His granddad waved him off. "I just think you and Lucy need Alice as much as she needs you."

Absurdly, Zach agreed. Despite the pitfalls, was he falling, just a little bit, in love with the gypsy woman?

A shiver of unexpected excitement raced up his spine. If he was—he wasn't saying he would give in to something that crazy—in the end it could turn out to be one of the most dicey things he'd ever done.

~ * ~

Lucy didn't want to miss even a second of Oaks Park during open hours, so the next morning, just before noon, Zach trailed behind the others while they walked to the park.

Acting weak and a little unstable on his feet, his granddad slipped a shaky hand in the crook of Alice's arm, earning him the concerned look the old coot was after. Lucy hung onto his other hand.

Zach hid a smirk. He'd seen this shaky old man act before when his granddad wanted something badly. There was nothing wrong with the octogenarian that a large scoop of his favorite strawberry ice cream wouldn't fix. Nonetheless, the three taking up the width of the sidewalk ahead of him made a pretty picture. One that Alice would bring to magical life if she painted it.

She was wearing a dress again. Another version of the red-flowered one she'd been wearing when he first saw her. And those red tennis shoes.

He tugged at the neck of his tee-shirt. The sun was awfully

46

warm for an Oregon spring day.

Without the others noticing, he took a picture with his cell. Just in case it came up in conversation, and the woman occupying most of his thoughts decided it was time to put people she cared about in her paintings.

They were not far from the main gates when his grandfather spotted an empty bench facing the river and took a seat.

Wary speculation scampered briefly over Alice's face before being hidden. Zach thought he was starting to get the guarded woman. Like a prickly porcupine, she didn't like anyone getting too close. And was he in trouble, because all he wanted was to get inside her bristly defenses.

She sat beside his granddad, while Lucy stretched out on the grass, unusually patient for a kid who'd talked about nothing else all morning except going on the rides as soon as they got to the park.

Zach chose a spot beside his daughter where he could watch Alice's expressions.

"Beautiful view, ain't it?" his grandfather said too casually.

Alice leaned back in the bench, all the tension easing from her shoulders. For the first time since he'd seen her paintings the night before she smiled. "It is."

Following her gaze to the river, Zach tried to see his world as she did. The Willamette was peaceful today in direct contrast to the storm building in his chest. Dogs played along the stretch of grass, watched over by their owners. Across the gentle rippling of the river's sun-dappled surface, on the opposite bank, was a marina.

"See that red building over there on the end? A guy I play poker with owns it. He had a boat repair shop. Best one in town, too." His grandfather shaded his eyes. "He's retired, and it's empty now. Not in bad shape though."

Those were more words than his granddad usually spoke in one go-around. *What are you up to old man?*

Alice leaned forward on her knees, squinting toward the river. "What's he going to do with it?"

"Dunno. Sell it, I suppose."

Alice's pale brows drew together.

His conniving grandfather shot him a look that said, *lend me a hand here, would you?*

To give Alice a reason to stay? Maybe that was a good idea. Maybe it wasn't.

But it didn't matter. From what he'd seen in the short time he'd known her, Alice wouldn't change her mind about heading down the road to the next town. Give up her nomadic existence? Just because he was beginning to think she could make a good life in Sellwood? With him?

Not having much luck in the love department, mountains of caution kept him from opening the door to that scary future. While he refused to lose his head, his traitorous body was shouting, *go for it!*

Alice hadn't hidden her intentions. He'd be wise to remember how the love of his life walking out the door had felt the last time it'd happened. And not even for the prettiest green eyes he'd ever seen could he give up the life he'd carefully put together for Lucy. The most he and Alice could have was a brief, steamy affair that had disaster written all over it.

He shook his head, shooting a silent message back to his grandfather. *Not on your life, Granddad.*

But that didn't mean, in the short amount of time he had to spend with the enticing woman, he couldn't show her an uncomplicated, good time.

Chapter 7

Don't be a fool.

Alice let her inner critic loose hoping it would talk some sense into her foolish heart.

Just because John reminded her of her grandpa, she would not let the older man sitting next to her entice her to stay. He didn't know he was offering a dream that for as long as she could remember had always been just beyond her reach.

No one in their right mind fell in love in two days. And certainly not a girl who knew better. She was *not* thinking how much fun it would be to watch Lucy grow into a young woman. And she was *not* falling for the charms of Zach Barret!

Stick to the plan. Get your fuel pump. Fix the Duke. Get back on the road before you do something stupid, like get involved to the point where all you take away besides a fixed truck is a broken heart.

Been there, done that. Did not want seconds.

Still, she couldn't help but contemplate the empty building across the river. If there was enough space for a garage where she could fix old classics, and a studio above to paint in…it would be a dream come true, one she'd secretly harbored for some time.

Zach stood, pulling his daughter to her feet. "Is everyone ready to ride the Spider?"

Several hours later, while John and Lucy took their fifth ride on the Thunder Roller Coaster, Alice found a bench angled toward the river where she could wait for Zach to return with cotton candy. He'd discovered she'd never had any and had gone off to make sure she "didn't miss the most important part of the amusement park," as he put it.

The most important part had been spending the day with Zach and his family, but she couldn't quite bring herself to say that to the man who'd for his own reasons had taken charge of entertaining her for the day.

The idea of having a look at the building John had pointed out earlier had taken hold. She couldn't see it from where she sat. The sudden desire to look inside was insane. She didn't have the money to buy an empty building that wouldn't change her mind about the lifestyle she'd chosen, one that had become a habit now, and comfortable.

Zach handed over a large, pink swirl of sugar confection before joining her on the bench. "Are you sorry you came today?"

Hot desire replaced her skittish nerves. Not wanting to show how affected she was, Alice kept her burning face turned in the direction of the building pulling at her. "No. It's been fun."

His next words were unexpected. "It's too bad you have to leave."

She shook her head. Could he know she'd just been thinking, maybe just this once, she could stay longer than planned?

With the sun warming her from overhead, the heavenly

sweetness of the cotton candy melted on her tongue, promising the possibility of a future she'd never thought was hers to grab.

Don't be a fool.

She shifted uneasily on the bench, more words spilling out than she intended. "I'm not sure how– We moved around a lot when I was a kid. Then— Well, it didn't work out."

"What didn't work out?" Zach asked in a low, persuasive rumble.

She didn't want her ghosts catching up with her. It made her stomach twist into aching knots thinking about that time in her life. To keep her sanity, she'd learned to shove her past into a closet hidden in the deepest part of her mind so that after losing the most important thing in her life, she could go on living.

She wasn't always successful at keeping the past where it belonged. And it scared her a bit to unlock that door, giving the painful memories their freedom.

Could she be as brave as Zach was? He gave all of himself to Lucy and made being a single dad look so easy.

Maybe the memory wouldn't hurt so much if she told him, if she let her demons out into the light. Could she finally let go?

She didn't look at him. Her throat closed off her breath. "I um…was married once. And pregnant. I lost the baby. It was my fault. And then I wasn't married anymore."

Zach shifted beside her. Strong hands gripped her shoulders and gently turned her to face him. He took her cotton candy, propping it up in his now empty cola cup.

"What happened?" he asked softly.

She'd never talked about that dark day. Not even to her grandpa.

Chin sinking to her chest, tears spilled over the dam of her self-control. "I was fighting with George, slipped on the edge of a rug, and fell down the stairs. If I hadn't been arguing with him over something as stupid as which crib we were going to get for the baby, or if I'd been watching where I was going, it wouldn't have happened."

It was no use. She couldn't hold back the waves of pain suffocating her as much now as on the day the doctor had told them their baby was dead.

Firm fingers lifted her chin. Zach's thumbs carefully wiped away the tears. His searching gaze held her in place. Alice's heart shuttered, then stopped beating for half a second.

"You tripped over a rug and fell down a flight of stairs, so your husband blamed you and left."

Her irresponsibility...her carelessness with the most important thing in her life sounded so much worse when he stated the facts like that. Alice slipped further into her self-loathing.

She hated herself. He should too.

Needing to get the whole ugly story out, she whispered, "While I was in the hospital. He said he didn't want to look at me. When I got home, all his things were gone."

Zach did the most unexpected thing. He pressed a kiss to her forehead. "And you've been living with this pain, by yourself, ever since?"

Confused by his reaction, the rest of her story stumbled out. "My grandpa wanted me to stay with him, but—" *I wouldn't let him help.*

Why hadn't she let him? He had a new wife, and a new life, that was why. Nice as Betty was, home wasn't with her grandpa. She didn't have a home anymore.

"George was wrong. It wasn't your fault. Sometimes bad things just happen." He leaned his forehead against hers. "And if George loved you, as upset as he was, he wouldn't have left you when you needed him most."

The tight band in her chest damming her emotions broke. Alice choked on a half-sob. Before she knew what was happening, Zach's arms wrapped around her pulling her into a safe harbor where she completely lost it. She cried for her lost motherhood, for the little girl who didn't get the chance to grow up and sell lemonade with her friends, for the impossible-to-scale walls she'd erected so she couldn't be hurt like that again.

"Shhhh. It's okay," Zach's soothing whisper rumbled in his chest.

She leaned back to see his face. "You don't hate me?"

Keeping his gaze locked on hers, he shook his head. "No." Blue eyes turned hard as glass. "If I was going to hate anyone it would be George."

Alice wasn't sure she believed Zach's assertion she wasn't at fault, but for the first time since that horrifying fall down the stairs, the burden of her grief lightened.

Slowly, giving her a chance to move away if she wanted, his lips covered hers, gently probing, encouraging her to accept the comfort he offered.

Forgetting where she was, she wrapped her arms around his neck and gave in to the sweetness of the kiss. He gently anchored her in a world that had completely spun in the opposite direction. She'd thought she knew where she stood, that she was okay with painting as she put the miles behind her. Suddenly she wasn't so sure anymore. And it was all because of this man who offered understanding and comfort she hadn't sought for herself.

In that moment of partial forgiveness, she wanted Zach more than she wanted anything else. And she didn't care who knew it.

Somewhere outside the bubble, in a world not taken over by the comfort turning into something else much more potent, came the sound of someone clearing her throat. By the third time, each *ahem* louder and closer than the one before, Alice finally broke away to find Lucy's laughing grin.

"The Roller Coaster is so cool. I could ride it all day." The girl plopped on the bench on Alice's other side.

John gave Zach an *atta-boy* slap on the shoulder and sent a wink in her direction.

Embarrassment flushed Alice's cheeks with heat. Okay, she did care.

Damn it! What had she done?

Chapter 8

Sleep was clearly overrated, so Alice got up, threw on a robe and slippers, and marched herself to the kitchen. The house was quiet, as it should be at five o'clock in the morning. She opened cupboards and gathered ingredients until she had all she wanted.

On the way home from Oaks Park they'd picked up Thai food. She'd eaten what she could, then quickly escaped to the garage to finish the tune-up on the van. No one had followed her, thank goodness, and by the time she'd returned to the house, they'd all gone to bed. Except she could hear Zach's deep voice as he made calls from his attic office.

Awake most of the night, the one thing she hadn't been able to get off her mind had been Zach's kiss. He'd only meant to offer comfort, but he *had* kissed her. Twice. Well, three times. Not an isn't-this-fun-but-I'm-not-serious brush of the lips, but knock-her-socks-off, blow-her-mind, game-changer kisses.

And while that in and of itself was enough to give a girl a

sleepless night, she couldn't escape the fact that she'd told him the one deepest, darkest secret she hadn't told anyone. Why had she done that?

If his kiss after was anything to go by, he didn't hate her. The man who'd wholeheartedly taken on the role of single dad didn't blame her for the loss of her child.

Was Zach right? She'd blamed herself for so long. Could she forgive her part in her baby girl's death?

Alice didn't know what to do. Except bake. That's what she used to do, back in the day when life was simpler before she'd gotten pregnant, then married, then not pregnant or married anymore.

She needed to take a step back from the man ringing more than her chimes, so she put on coffee to brew and started mixing ingredients to the chocolate chip cookies recipe she knew by heart. And was grateful. The pain of losing her baby wasn't gone, but it didn't feel as heavy.

"You're up early. What are you cooking?" The deep sleepy voice spun Alice around in surprise.

Rumpled hair, discerning eyes still half asleep, his robe gaped revealing a light sprinkle of hair on his chest.

Oh, man! She liked this guy. Maybe even loved.

"I'm making cookies." A little lightheaded, she tried not to stare at the point at which the robe's tie was knotted low on his hips. Just a little bit lower and she would see more of Zach than would be good for either of them.

"And coffee. Bless you." He reached for the coffee pot. "Couldn't sleep?"

"It happens occasionally." She shrugged, trying not to see what was hidden beneath the recalcitrant robe. "Sorry if I woke you."

"Been having trouble in the sleeping department myself." His voice took on an alert, soft note of invitation. An invitation that was far too tempting.

Alice couldn't go there. Nothing in her life had prepared her to trust a stranger's intentions. Except Zach Barret wasn't a stranger. Not anymore.

Shoulders tight, hands clammy, she finished mixing the dough and dropped spoonfuls onto the baking sheet. When was she going to let go of the past and see what kind of future she could have?

Embarrassed, her gaze avoiding his, she put the sheet of rounded mounds of cookie dough in the oven. "I'm um...sorry about yesterday."

"Sorry about what?"

Waving a hand, she tried to make light of it. "Oh you know, blubbering all over your shirt. The kissing."

She'd turned to drag out another baking sheet so didn't realize he'd come close enough to back her into a corner of the counter.

"No problem." He pushed a stray strand of hair behind her ear. "I didn't mind."

Alice cleared her throat. "Mind?"

Those kissable lips turned up into a smile, while something more powerful she wasn't sure she wanted to name glinted at her from the sharp blue of his eyes. "I didn't mind the blubbering. Or the kissing."

"That's good. I kind of worried you might have felt put on the spot, or that you felt obligated in some way, and I just wanted you to know, that's not what I intended," she babbled. Taking a breath to calm down, she motioned for him to move aside. Her voice shook, but she didn't care, just desperately wanted to change the subject. "So what are you doing today?"

He followed her lead. Moved. Gave her room to breathe. "Working on orders. A friend of Granddad's is in the hospital. She owns Gram's Treasures in fact, which explains why it was closed the other day. He's going to visit her and see if he can lend a hand with her store while she's out of commission. And Lucy has a play date and sleep-over at Carla's house. If I take advantage of the peace and quiet, I can get a good share of the mountain done."

Was that a hint not to bother him? The excitement building in her belly deflated.

"You?" he asked almost too casually.

Keeping her eyes pinned on his handsome face, Alice silently snorted at her own expense. Of course, he didn't want to get involved with her. She was an employee with one foot hovering over the gas pedal. And he wasn't the kind of guy who did short-term, hot, and heavy bed exercises. Which was one of the reasons she liked him so much, damn it.

But his kisses had whetted her appetite, and his open robe had given her ideas she was having trouble ignoring. "I'll be earning the wage you're paying me by baking these cookies. And if you're lucky I'll make bacon and eggs, and cinnamon rolls for breakfast. Then I have work to finish on the van."

In her attempt to put distance between them, she'd mostly finished the van last night, but there were one or two things left to do.

Refilling his coffee cup, he gestured haphazardly at the stairs that led to the upper floors. "I'd better get back to it. How long before breakfast?"

"An hour?"

"Perfect."

Alice listened to his footsteps going upstairs and ran her

fingers through her hair to pull it off her face. She was in trouble. Big, big trouble. What was she going to do? Pretend the man didn't attract her as much as he did, that's what.

Easier said than done, a little voice in her head snickered.

The next best thing then, barring any other complications was to pick up the fuel pump as early tomorrow morning as possible, fix the Duke, repack her clothes in her overnight bag, and hit the road before the sun started to set.

All she had to do between now and then was keep her mitts to herself and off the very sexy Zach Barret.

Chapter 9

Distracted, Zach pushed away from his desk, another order finished, three more large ones to go.

So you kissed the woman, he scoffed. He'd wanted to kiss her. See how she tasted. Find out if the uber-independent woman would melt in his arms. And she had. With flying colors. Holding Alice, her heart breaking over her loss, had kicked the legs right out from under him. She'd wanted her baby. More than anything. *His* world might never be the same.

The contrast between Alice and his ex, Janet, rocked Zach's notion of who he thought Alice was – a girl, alone in the world, who didn't know how to put down roots. Thinking of her paintings, he understood now why they were bereft of children.

The hungry look in her eyes earlier, when they'd landed on his bare chest, lingering longer than was socially polite, nearly had him laughing and made him a little faint because suddenly he realized, it would be so easy to give the beautiful nomad his heart.

He'd never been a big hit with the ladies. Inexplicably, with

Alice, he wanted to put himself out there and see if something could come of the sparks exploding between them.

Mouth-watering smells of frying bacon drifted up to his office.

Shaking his head at his recklessness, but wanting to ask Alice out on a movie date, he scrubbed his eyes with his palms. When he dropped his hands to his desk the woman disrupting his peaceful, very full existence stood on the landing into his office.

The keeping-my-distance look on her pretty face didn't welcome an impromptu invitation. Yet, here he was, standing, toes hanging over the edge of a precipice, considering diving into dangerous depths anyway.

"There's no hot water."

Of course, there wasn't. "The hot water tank's been acting up. I was hoping it would hang on for a while longer."

When she studied him, seemingly searching for conversation, he said, "I'll take care of it."

She nodded before turning to retrace her steps – reluctantly it seemed. He hoped. "Breakfast is ready. Lucy and your grandfather have already started."

Dressed in black leggings, a red and black paisley tunic top that hugged her waist, and the red tennis shoes, she took his breath away and made him stupid. "You want to go to a movie tonight?"

He'd crossed to the landing, but she was already halfway down the stairs. She stopped but didn't look at him. "I don't think that's such a good idea."

He descended a step toward her, his boots scraping the wood. "Nothing serious. Just two friends enjoying the newest hit film together."

Shoulders rigid, she resumed her descent. "I don't know."

"You'll be doing me a huge favor. After working all day, I'll need a break," he said, following at a good distance so he didn't scare off the woman, or himself. It was a big risk he was taking. "Think about it?"

She glanced over her shoulder and hesitated. The tension eased from her expressive eyes.

"Okay." A half-smile curled one corner of her mouth, and unaccountably Zach felt like a million bucks.

When they entered the kitchen with its breakfast smells and warm sunshine coming in the window over the sink, he wasn't thinking about getting Alice into his bed – at least not much – but he was hoping, for one night, to give her something she didn't presently have. A night out on the town with a friend who could give her peace from the secret she'd held so close to her chest.

The loneliness he sensed in her paintings has its roots in grief. Alice needed more in her life than an endless road and jobs that didn't last long enough to encourage her to stay and make a home of her own.

Listening to her laugh at his grandfather's and Lucy's jokes, Zach wolfed down the best cinnamon roll he'd ever tasted. He silently groaned over the perfection of the pastry and the woman who'd made it, wondering if he should have a second.

Worse, for the first time since his daughter's birth, watching the emotions playing across Alice's face, her eyes crinkled with laughter one minute, round with a good dose of uneasiness the next, he figured it out. The delightful and beautiful Alice York could be happy with them if she would give them a chance.

One would think the thought of his family becoming complete with the addition of the skittish woman would scare the logical, pragmatic businessman right out of him. But surprisingly, it didn't. For a mystifying reason, he wanted to give her what he had. A home to always come home to.

"Why did the elephant cross the road?" Lucy asked Alice.

Alice shook her head as she stacked dishes on the counter.

"Because the chicken couldn't be bothered," Lucy shouted, jumping out of her seat, nearly tripping on her own feet as she laughed herself silly.

Alice cracked up too.

That was it. He was a goner. Any woman who'd laugh at his daughter's crazy jokes was the one for him. Besides, he'd told Lucy that one, so by extension, she was laughing at his crazy joke. Now if he could just get her to take in a movie with him.

His granddad pushed back from the table. "I'm off to the hospital to see Lois. Then I'm helping with the *Ghosts That Haunt Portland* tour. After, I'm meeting Buck and Betty at the airport. We'll take the shuttle home, so don't wait up."

"What time does their flight arrive?"

"After midnight."

Alice looked his way, brows rising in question, a shockingly intimate, silent moment of communication that was natural for couples who'd been together a long time, not a man and woman who'd only known each other three days.

"Buck and Betty have been visiting their new great-grand-baby," he answered her silent query.

Zach joined her at the sink to help with the dishes, and since there was no hot water, put some in a pot to boil on the stove. The domestic wave washing over him rocked every notion he had about falling in love. Slowly. Taking his time to get to know the woman capturing his heart.

How in the heck had he and Alice gone from zero to sixty in the short time they'd been acquainted?

Desperate for some distance from his unnerving thoughts, Zach interrogated his daughter. "Luce, do you have your overnight bag packed?"

"Yup."

"Do you have the money I gave you for the rest of your school supplies?"

"Yesss, Dad." He gave her a stern, watch-your-manners look. She gave him an aggrieved sigh back. "In my backpack."

Stopping on her way to her room, uncertainty clouded her young face. The manners he'd worked so hard to teach the only girl in his life thus far won out. "I could help clean up."

His little girl was growing up. A little sad at the prospect of her childhood passing right before his eyes, he shooed her away. "I've got this covered. Go be with your friends."

When Lucy returned shouldering her backpack, she took the banana he held out, hesitated briefly, then looked from him to Alice and asked, "What are you doing today?"

They could be mother and daughter. What a shame they weren't.

Zach took the opportunity to take over dishwashing duties while he shamelessly listened. Ordinary question, an ordinary day, but somehow brighter than its predecessors because Alice was part of it.

In the end, getting a date with the coolest girl passing through town wasn't as difficult as he'd thought it would be.

"Well, I have to finish up the van and clean up the garage." Alice took a deep breath. "After that, your dad and I are going to see a movie."

Lucy's eyes grew big. "Really?

Alice laughed.

A hot hunger took a triumphant somersault in his belly.

Chapter 9

"Really." Alice flashed him a slow smile, the pretty rose-colored blush climbing to her sculpted cheeks cinching the deal.

Zach Barret had a new girl in his life. All he had to do was convince that girl to unpack her traveling bag and abandon her wandering ways.

Chapter 10

Waiting for Zach to return with drinks and popcorn, Alice marveled—here she was on an old-fashioned date in a theater that had first opened its doors in 1926. The Moreland Theater still retained the bygone era's feel and sensibility, just like the classic vehicles she loved to work on.

As the lights dimmed, excited anticipation tied her up in knots. She hadn't been on many real "dates". The few times she'd tried dating after George left her in the hospital had been complete flops. It didn't take long to figure out, finding a guy who would be reliable, and who wouldn't run when the going got tough; a man whose only solution wasn't to leave her behind, would never happen.

Zach sat next to her and handed her a cola. Propping a large container of popcorn on his knee, he leaned close to whisper, "Did I miss anything?"

"No," she whispered back, a little tongue-tied.

She hadn't seen him all day, working in the garage and on the van, admittedly avoiding the man who inexplicably attracted her like Anthony did Cleopatra. Now, there was a relationship that had ended badly.

Disturbed by how she'd spent the entire day thinking of the man she was avoiding, and then spending more time than necessary dressing to catch his eye, Alice gulped her drink. The sweet liquid hit the back of her throat, choking her until she lost her breath.

Zach shifted, patting her on the back. "Are you okay?"

Eyes watering, she nodded. A few more coughs and she could breathe again.

Subtle light from the movie lit his handsome face revealing concern she wasn't accustomed to. She knew how to take care of herself and hadn't needed someone to manage that department in a long time.

His arm settled around her shoulder. Could she live in the moment, and enjoy being fussed over just a little? At least until she left anyway. Who knew when she'd get another chance to go out with a good-looking guy, who if she was being honest, ticked all her must-have boxes.

She sighed with something close to contentment. For tonight, she'd indulge herself in Zach Barret. Leaning into his shoulder, she said, "I'm fine."

His slow, sexy smile started her on a roller-coaster ride that took her through the movie about two teenagers with cancer who against all the odds fell in love—a love that came with no guarantees. The twist at the end had Alice digging in her pack purse for tissue to wipe the tears from her face.

Zach tugged her close to his chest. "God. I'm so sorry. I didn't mean—I should have picked a different movie."

"That was so good," Alice said at the same time with a watery laugh.

He pressed a kiss to her forehead. "It was."

Surprised, she glanced up and found eyes shining with the same amazement rolling through her.

"Ready to go home? Or do you want to stop for a drink?"

Home?

That he was worried how his choice in movies had affected her, and because he was giving her a choice, and she had all these *feelings* boiling inside needing an outlet—

"Your house," she croaked out. But then fear pushed her too—what if she liked being in his bed—so she added. "No strings."

The blue of his eyes deepening with simmering heat, he laced their fingers together and agreed, "No strings."

It might be a mistake, stealing one night with Zach, but like the girl in the film, she couldn't say no.

They made it through the front door before the tension building during the short walk from the theater broke. Alice was nervous. Sex was like riding a bike, right? Once you knew how, you never forgot? At least that's what she hoped as Zach's hard body pressed her back against the hardwood of the door.

Evidence of his arousal caught her breath. "I…um…haven't done this in a long time."

"Me, neither," he whispered against the curve of her neck, sending a quiver of excitement over her skin.

His lips captured her, settling in for a thorough exploration. Lips, tongues, and then eager hands skimmed over her feminine curves until they pulled the straps of her sundress down her arms.

"I love this dress." The words were a groan across her lips as though he'd become drunk on her. Slowly he dropped the dress to the floor, revealing only bare skin.

Her breath hitched, tangling with his groan of appreciation.

"Beautiful," he whispered, taking his time, looking, molding, tongue laving, mouth sucking with hungry pressure that had her making short work of the buttons on his shirt.

Wrenching the garment downward until he let her remove it, she flung the cotton to the floor. Slow foreplay working up to the crescendo of wild sex might have worked for her once upon a time, but not tonight. She wanted Zach Barrett. Now. This second.

He made her feel…wanted. No more being a good girl and waiting.

"More," she demanded against the delicious man's lips.

Kissing him deeply, she reveled in the strong arms wrapping around her with a strength that was new in her experience. Stomachs mashed together, the hard length of him oh-so-close, Alice pushed until he gave her the space she needed to dispense with his belt and shirt.

The desperate need to intimately connect with *this* man—no other would do she realized—was crazy. Wasn't it? Why here? Why now? Because he'd seen inside her tangled mess and not been scared off? Because he was the man who could fill the empty holes in her life? The one she'd thought didn't exist?

"Wait," he gasped, reaching into his pocket to pull out a foil packet.

Banishing her confusion, she laughed. "Were you that sure where tonight was headed?"

His grin was cocky. "A guy is always hopeful."

Grabbing his face with both hands, she drew him with her as she leaned against the door. "So is a girl."

Fingers pressed gently against her lips. "Hold that thought."

Bare seconds later he'd finished what she started and stood

strong and straight before her, his naked glory the most beautiful thing. She hadn't needed anyone in a long time, so she gave up trying to figure out the whys. She could accept she needed him. For this one night.

"Come here." Wrapping her fingers around his hard length, her thumb tested the responsiveness of the silky head.

His sex pumped in her hand. His grin turned wicked. "Yes, ma'am."

Lips molding to hers, Zach hitched her leg on his hip. Tongues explored and danced together as his long fingers eased aside her barely there panties and found her moist entrance.

His thumb circled her clit. Her hips bucked when he pushed inside.

"What do you want?" His gravelly voice, pure seduction, along with talented fingers, threatened to send Alice over the edge.

No one had ever asked her what she wanted. Breathing in his earthy spice scent, sliding her hand up and down his hard shaft, she gave him the only answer she could. "You."

He stopped long enough to put on the condom, then lifted her easily, so her legs circled his waist. Entering into her pulsing warmth with an excruciating slowness, he drove her nearly mad with her body's demand to have him. Completely. Inside.

Scraping her nails along his back, she ordered, panting, "In. Now."

"Patience, love."

Centimeter by excruciatingly slow centimeter, he joined them, sucking first on her lower lip, gently biting his way down her neck, taking one breast, then the next so deep in his arousing mouth, Alice had no thought left but the orgasm building to a tsunami.

She keened as the riptide hit her. Zach pumped hard, harder

and harder until he joined her, and the wild, mind-blowing wave took her away again.

Barely able to catch her breath, she leaned her forehead against his. "Oh my."

He laughed a deep pleased-with-himself rumble that reignited her slow burn. "We're not done yet, beautiful lady."

She arched her brows in disbelief and had a spike of hope he wasn't kidding. "No?"

"No." That promise was delivered in a suddenly serious vow as she fell into the blue wells of his eyes, he carried her upstairs to his bedroom.

~ * ~

"Come here, love." Zach spooned around Alice's back, drawing her so close not even a piece of thin paper would fit between them.

Love? Shock slithered like a sneaky snake in her belly.

His foot rubbed hers, slowly back and forth, not lessening the truth. She was nobody's love. Never had been.

When his palm and fingers splayed across her belly and his breath deepened in sleep, panic slowly ebbed, only to resurface in dreams of a phantom Zach packing his bags and leaving her over and over.

She woke with a start, tired and disoriented, to an early rising sun peeking through the window. At first, she wasn't sure where she was. A heavy arm wrapped her waist. Legs tangled with hers. A soft snore whispered in her ear.

The previous night came back in a breathless rush. She was in Zach's bed.

Alice blushed at the number of times he'd shattered her senses. Never had a man been so attuned to her needs, and then pandered to them as though her enjoyment was all he wanted in the whole world. Certainly not George, who was a slam-bam-thank-you-ma'am kind of guy.

The afterglow faded as she remembered how many times they'd done "it", and that softly whispered, *love*.

Heart pounding, her stomach twisted into a knot. He couldn't possibly have meant he loved her.

Easing out of the warm cocoon of his bed, the picture of his granddad tripping over their clothes on the way into the house covered her skin in embarrassed chills.

What had *she done?*

Tip-toeing to Zach's closet, she grabbed one of his shirts and hastily put it on.

A sleepy voice stopped her at the door. "Where are you going?"

Alice turned slowly, fingers fumbling as she buttoned the shirt.

"Alice?"

She took a deep breath and looked up. Zach sat on the side of the bed, the sheet draped over his lap, but just barely.

"I'm leaving."

"Right now?"

"Today."

Silence descended between them. He asked softly, "Why?"

She couldn't stop the rush of words. "We…I shouldn't have done this. I…I have the job in Longview. And…and I don't want to hurt you."

She sounded stupid, but what she'd started with Sexy Dad felt too much like she'd thrown a penny in a wishing well and asked for the impossible. Between her parents, her and George, and her grandpa, only her grandpa had been able to make love work. She refused to become the third failure out of four.

"I can't stay." Finally, she choked out, "I don't know how."

Which made her the villain she'd always hated.

Zach pulled on sweats that hung low on his hips, giving her a show that would have changed her mind if she'd given the scary emotions inside half a chance. He moved toward her, but she held up her hand to stop him.

"The truth is I'm not like you. I failed to keep my family together. Twice. I can't fail you, too. It would kill me."

"We can work it out. I promise. I love you."

"You love my ankles," she tried to joke. He'd mentioned it once, or three times while they were making love. When he didn't laugh, she said, "Then you're a fool."

He took a step toward her. "If I am, I'm a happy fool."

Before he could touch her, she reached for the door. "I'm not brave, Zach."

"I think you are." Hands dropping to his sides, he stayed where he was. "What will I tell Lucy? And Granddad?"

"Tell them…I'll miss them."

Chapter 11

Alice was gone by mid-morning. Zach didn't try to stop her. The wobble in her voice, the determined lift of her chin, and the resignation in her gorgeous eyes tied his hands. He watched through the window as she drove off.

When she hesitated, glancing toward the house before climbing into the cab, he thought she'd changed her mind. Every moment they'd spent together, Alice laughing with Lucy, riding the rides with him at Oaks Park, her telling him about her lost baby and marriage, the heat of their lovemaking, it all played through his mind like a fast-rolling reel of film.

But she didn't stay. She got in her truck and drove away.

He banged his fist on the wall, clenching his jaw at the painful reverberation up his arm. Zach hung his head, working harder than he had on anything to get a grip on the tangled ball of frustration, anger, and regret growing too big for his chest. How could he be so stupid and fall for a girl who couldn't or wouldn't give them a chance?

Men didn't cry, but if they did, he'd be howling like a baby.

Alice was right. He *was* a fool.

His granddad spoke behind him. "When we got home last night, looked like you and Alice had a bit of a party going on."

Zach spun to face his granddad's silly grin.

"I put your clothes in the laundry room so Lucy wouldn't trip over them. No point in giving the child ideas before they come to her naturally."

And speaking of his child. Lucy came in the front door wearing a fierce scowl. "Where's Alice going?"

Zach's throat tightened. "She had to go to her job in Longview."

"Why?" His daughter's voice wobbled. "What did you say to her to make her leave?"

He shoved his hands in his jeans pockets. His daughter deserved the truth. "I told her I love her."

Tears started down his daughter's cheeks. "She didn't say goodbye."

"She wanted to," he lied through clenched teeth.

He reached to hug his daughter, but with a strangled sob Lucy shrugged him off and ran to her room.

This was why...he'd known better...Lucy's happiness was all that mattered, and he'd screwed up. He'd fallen in love with another girl who didn't think twice about leaving what was most important behind. When was he going to learn?

His granddad clapped him sympathetically on the shoulder. "So you're just going to let her go, son?"

If he was a sailor—or Alice—he'd be cursing up a blue streak.

No, he wasn't going to let her get off that easily. There had been a moment after they'd made love when she'd snuggled into the crook of his arm, her soft hair tickling his chin, when his world had stopped wobbling. She was humming softly. Like her world had stopped wobbling too. She probably didn't even know the happy sound was vibrating quietly through her body, leaking into his chest, giving a lift to his pulse.

Something miraculously close to contentment had settled around his heart. He was in love with the most improbable, stubborn woman. "I don't know if I can convince her to come back."

His granddad grinned widely. "You'll think of something."

The next morning, after a lengthy phone call, he'd worked out a plan. He found Lucy out back on the swing. She'd been too quiet since Alice's departure, her sad face a fraction of the ache that had replaced his miraculous contentment.

He took the second swing, silently rocking back and forth with her for a moment.

Lucy broke her silence. "How come Alice didn't want to stay with us?"

Sometimes adult behavior was difficult to explain, but he gave it a shot. "I think she wanted to but is afraid."

"Why?"

"Well." He took a deep breath. "I think she hasn't had anyone she can rely on like you and Granddad and I rely on each other. So it's hard for her to trust anyone."

"Like when we first moved here and I didn't know anyone and I was scared to go to a new school?"

"Exactly."

"We can't let her go. We have to find her and tell her not to be scared."

"I'm going to, but I need you to do me a favor."

Lucy jumped off the swing. "What?"

"I need you to stay with Granddad."

"But I want to come with you!"

He hugged her tight. "I know you do, but when a guy asks a lady to marry him, it's something he has to do on his own."

Her eyes grew round. "You're going to ask Alice to marry you?"

"If that's okay with you."

"OMG, Dad! Yes! She'd be the best mom."

"I can't promise she'll say yes," he warned his child. And himself. "But I have to try, even if she ends up saying no. Life doesn't always give us what we want, but that doesn't mean we shouldn't try. Know what I'm saying, baby girl?"

Lucy chewed on her thumbnail. "Like the first time I rode the roller-coaster at Oaks Park? I was so afraid, but you said I wouldn't know how brave I could be if I didn't try."

"Yes, just like that."

"So you're going to be brave?

He pulled her into a bear hug and kissed the top of her head. "The bravest I can be."

"Then she'll say yes. I know she will."

Zach wished he could be as sure. Alice had stubborn down pat when it came to keeping everyone at arm's length. Her barriers were built high and wide, but he wouldn't let that deter him.

He and Lucy's mom hadn't worked hard enough to stay together. The love just hadn't been there.

With Alice, he'd lost his heart, probably from that first glimpse of her ankles. This time he was going to fight tooth and nail for what he wanted. And what he wanted was to wake up to Alice in his bed every day.

After a quick stop to pick up his surprise, he hit the road, heading north to Longview.

It took three tries, but he finally spotted her truck parked in the lot of Dave's Classic Restorations. The back door to her gypsy canopy was open. He could see movement inside.

His stomach twisting into a nervous knot, he parked nearby.

God help him, his hands were shaking. Rubbing them on his pants, he grabbed the papers and the dozen red roses he'd picked up on his way out of Sellwood.

Alice came out just as he reached the Ford. Her eyes went round with surprise. "How did you find me?"

"There are three shops in Longview that specialize in classic cars. This was the third one on my list."

Happily, he lost himself in the warm green depths staring at him in disbelief and hope all rolled into one. "I can't believe you're here."

Holding out the vivid roses that reminded him so much of the woman who'd turned his life upside down and awakened his heart, he took a step closer, blurting, "I want you to marry me."

He wasn't sure she'd take the roses, but she did and buried her nose in the crimson-red petals.

"Will you marry me?"

"You don't even know me. You can't possibly want to marry me."

"I know you, Alice York. You're brave. An adventure on wheels. You have a warm heart. I love you." He dared to cup her cheek. "Marry me."

Closing her eyes, she leaned into his hand. "How do I know you won't stop loving me in a year, or five, or ten?"

Her voice was small, unsure. If he hadn't already been head-over-heels in love with her, his heart would have taken the plunge right then.

"I give you my word, I'll always love you. And I will never

leave you. We'll put it in our will, they have to bury us in the same coffin."

She gave a watery laugh.

Tucking the hand holding the roses behind her back, Zach planted a kiss on Alice he hoped would show this woman of his heart how much they belonged together. Two seconds in, he wanted more. Much more.

Against her lips, he asked, "Can we move this inside your truck?"

"I don't know," she said, but her eyes said something different. They sparkled, and she gifted him with a knee-buckling smile.

"How big is your bed?"

"I can throw blankets on the floor—"

He backed her up a step and saw the painting on her easel. "You've been painting."

Her gaze strayed to the somber merry-go-round where she'd added Lucy, Carla, and Tiffany in bright, vibrant colors. "Yes. It's finally finished."

The tight band around his chest popped loose. "Now you have to marry me."

Her expression lost some of its caution. "I'm not any good at marriage, Zach. Are you sure?"

"Absolutely sure. Say yes."

When she still hesitated, he told her, "I'm not a quitter, love. Lucy and Granddad will vouch for me. I won't quit on you."

The worry and fear pinching her pale face dissipated like fog in bright rays of sunlight.

He kissed her long and hard before whispering again. "Say yes."

She took a deep breath, the corners of her smile trembling. "Yes."

Wanting to shout to the world how much he loved Alice York, Zach handed over his second gift.

"What's this?"

"An early wedding present." He studied the finished painting at her back. It was so full of light, and life, and love. And he had just the place to hang it in the house.

"A bill of sale with my name on it?"

"For the building on the river. On the first floor, you can restore classic cars. The second can be your studio." He took the papers from her and propped them on the narrow window ledge. The roses ended up next to the easel. Pulling her close so she nestled safely in his arms, he said with conviction, "We'll grow old together. Have more babies, if that's what you want. Either way, I'll cherish every second of every day we have together."

"I love you Zach Barret," she whispered. "When do we start?"

"Now." And he sealed their first step into a bright future with a kiss that promised she'd finally come home.

About the Author

I admit right up front, I got the nomad bug at an early age. Because of that, I collect way too much useless information. I have a large home library and I love to write bold, brave, heartwarming stories. An award-winning author, I write contemporary romance, women's fiction, and romantic fantasy. Luckily, I'm easily bribed with an intriguing story and a good cup of coffee. When not writing in my home office, my favorite things are spending time with family and friends, traveling, reading, watching movies, gardening, taking pictures of nature and architectural marvels, and remodeling the house that after thirty years, is finally starting to feel like home. I would love it if you followed me on social media.

You can connect with me on:

🌐 https://www.susanlute.com

f https://www.facebook.com/susanlute

🔗 https://www.facebook.com/SusanLuteBooks

🔗 https://www.instagram.com/authorsusanlute

🔗 https://www.pinterest.com/sidella

🔗 https://www.goodreads.com/author/show/1252907.Susan_
Lute

🔗 https://www.bookbub.com/authors/susan-lute

Subscribe to my newsletter:

✉ https://www.susanlute.com/newsletter

Also by Susan Lute

A Strawberry Ridge Romance **Coming September 2024**
　The Prodigal Brother Returns

Angel Point Romance Series
　The Sheriff's Baby Bargain
　Wanted by the Marshal
　The Christmas Makeover
　The Valentine Project
　The Fake Marriage Proposal

Sellwood Series
　A Merry Little Sellwood Christmas, A Sellwood Short
　Sealed With A Kiss
　Love Lessons

Falling For a Hero Series
　A Girl Named Jane
　Jane's Long March Home
　A Marine's Christmas Proposal, A Short Story

Rosewood Series
　The Return of Benjamin Quincy
　Be My Valentine? A Rosewood Short

The London Affair

The Broken Road

Oops...We're Married? A Silhouette Romance Classic